P9-DWI-074

THE BOXCAR CHILDREN
SURPRISE ISLAND
THE YELLOW HOUSE MYSTERY
MYSTERY RANCH
MIKE'S MYSTERY
BLUE BAY MYSTERY
THE WOODSHED MYSTERY
THE LIGHTHOUSE MYSTERY
MOUNTAIN TOP MYSTERY
SCHOOLHOUSE MYSTERY
CABOOSE MYSTERY
HOUSEBOAT MYSTERY
SNOWBOUND MYSTERY
TREE HOUSE MYSTERY
BICYCLE MYSTERY
MYSTERY IN THE SAND
MYSTERY BEHIND THE WALL
BUS STATION MYSTERY
BENNY UNCOVERS A MYSTERY
THE HAUNTED CABIN MYSTERY
THE DESERTED LIBRARY MYSTERY
THE ANIMAL SHELTER MYSTERY
THE OLD MOTEL MYSTERY
THE MYSTERY OF THE HIDDEN PAINTING
THE AMUSEMENT PARK MYSTERY
THE MYSTERY OF THE MIXED-UP ZOO
THE CAMP-OUT MYSTERY
THE MYSTERY GIRL
THE MYSTERY CRUISE
THE DISAPPEARING FRIEND MYSTERY
THE MYSTERY OF THE SINGING GHOST
THE MYSTERY IN THE SNOW
THE PIZZA MYSTERY
THE MYSTERY HORSE
THE MYSTERY AT THE DOG SHOW
THE CASTLE MYSTERY
THE MYSTERY OF THE LOST VILLAGE
THE MYSTERY ON THE ICE
THE MYSTERY OF THE PURPLE POOL
THE GHOST SHIP MYSTERY
THE MYSTERY IN WASHINGTON, DC
THE CANOE TRIP MYSTERY

THE MYSTERY OF THE HIDDEN BEACH
THE MYSTERY OF THE MISSING CAT
THE MYSTERY AT SNOWFLAKE INN
THE MYSTERY ON STAGE
THE DINOSAUR MYSTERY
THE MYSTERY OF THE STOLEN MUSIC
THE MYSTERY AT THE BALL PARK
THE CHOCOLATE SUNDAE MYSTERY
THE MYSTERY OF THE HOT AIR BALLOON
THE MYSTERY BOOKSTORE
THE PILGRIM VILLAGE MYSTERY
THE MYSTERY OF THE STOLEN BOXCAR
THE MYSTERY IN THE CAVE
THE MYSTERY ON THE TRAIN
THE MYSTERY AT THE FAIR
THE MYSTERY OF THE LOST MINE
THE GUIDE DOG MYSTERY
THE HURRICANE MYSTERY
THE PET SHOP MYSTERY
THE MYSTERY OF THE SECRET MESSAGE
THE FIREHOUSE MYSTERY
THE MYSTERY IN SAN FRANCISCO
THE NIAGARA FALLS MYSTERY
THE MYSTERY AT THE ALAMO
THE OUTER SPACE MYSTERY
THE SOCCER MYSTERY
THE MYSTERY IN THE OLD ATTIC
THE GROWLING BEAR MYSTERY
THE MYSTERY OF THE LAKE MONSTER
THE MYSTERY AT PEACOCK HALL
THE WINDY CITY MYSTERY
THE BLACK PEARL MYSTERY
THE CEREAL BOX MYSTERY
THE PANTHER MYSTERY
THE MYSTERY OF THE QUEEN'S JEWELS
THE STOLEN SWORD MYSTERY
THE BASKETBALL MYSTERY
THE MOVIE STAR MYSTERY
THE MYSTERY OF THE PIRATE'S MAP
THE GHOST TOWN MYSTERY
THE MYSTERY OF THE BLACK RAVEN
THE MYSTERY IN THE MALL

The Boxcar Children Mysteries

THE MYSTERY OF THE EMPTY SAFE

created by
GERTRUDE CHANDLER WARNER

Illustrated by Charles Tang

Albert Whitman & Company
Chicago, Illinois

Contents

CHAPTER 1

A Party — With a Surprise

"I say chocolate!" said six-year-old Benny Alden.

"How about vanilla with purple filling," his ten-year-old sister, Violet, suggested. Purple was her favorite color.

"Alex wanted a strawberry cake, so that's what it's going to be," said their twelve-year-old sister, Jessie.

"Remember, this party is for Alex, so we have to do it the way he wants it," fourteen-year-old Henry reminded his brother and sisters.

The Alden children had just started their own birthday party company. Their friend Alex Pierce was turning eight, and his parents had hired the Aldens to run his party. They knew Alex liked dinosaurs, so the whole party was going to be about dinosaurs. The Aldens were on their way to the store to buy all the supplies they'd need.

Jessie, who was very organized, had written everything down. "The party is going to be this Saturday at three o'clock," she said, reading from a piece of paper. "We'll make dinosaur decorations to put on the walls. We'll play a bunch of games about dinosaurs. At the end we'll have the cake, which we'll make in the shape of a *Tyrannosaurus rex*," Jessie said. "And it will be a *strawberry* cake," she added, looking at Benny and Violet.

"Oh, all right," Benny agreed.

"I've got the money Mrs. Pierce gave us for supplies," Henry said, patting his pocket.

"Here's a good place to put up one of our posters," Violet said as they passed a bulletin board that said GREENFIELD NEWS at the top. She held up a sign that read:

THE ALDENS' BIRTHDAY PARTY COMPANY
HIRE US FOR A GREAT TIME!
WE'LL DO ALL THE PLANNING AND THE CLEANUP.
CALL 555-0434

The Aldens had made little tags at the bottom with their phone number. That way people could tear off a tag and take the Aldens' number with them if they were interested.

The children lived with their grandfather, James Alden, because their parents had died. At first they had been afraid Mr. Alden would be mean, so they'd run away from him. They'd found an old boxcar in the woods and had gone to live there. But when at last they'd met their grandfather, they found he was a good, kind man. They came to live with him in his big house. And he brought their boxcar to the backyard so they could still play in it when they wanted to.

As they walked through the streets of Greenfield, the children put up their posters on telephone poles and bulletin boards, and in store windows when the store owners said it was okay. Most store owners were happy to help the hardworking kids.

A few minutes later the Aldens were entering Party Time, a new store in Greenfield. Party Time was filled with everything you could possibly need for a party: all different kinds of decorations, party hats and blowers, paper plates and tablecloths, and small toys that could be given away as party favors. There were also paper, paints, and markers, so that people could make their own decorations. The Aldens picked out streamers and balloons, and large sheets of paper and paints to paint pictures of dinosaurs.

"Hey, look at these!" Benny cried when he saw a bin filled with tiny plastic dinosaurs. "They will make great party favors."

When they were done, the children took

their purchases to the front counter. A pretty young woman greeted them. "Are you kids planning a party?" she asked, taking their items out of the basket one by one.

"Yes, we are," said Henry.

"It's a dinosaur party!" Benny shouted.

"Cool," the woman said with a smile.

"We have our own party company!" Benny told her.

"You know, we should put up one of our posters here," Jessie pointed out, pulling a poster from her backpack and handing it to the woman. "Do you have a place we could put this?"

The woman took the poster and read it. "Are you the Aldens?" she asked.

"Yes, I'm Henry, and these are my sisters and brother, Jessie, Violet, and Benny," Henry said.

"I'm Patti Fox. Pleased to meet you!" She stuck out her hand and shook the children's hands. "I'd be happy to put up your sign right here next to the register, where everyone will see it as they come in." She tacked the poster up next to one advertising a ma-

gician named Cassandra the Great. "How did you get the idea to start a party service?" Ms. Fox asked.

"We like to plan parties and bake cakes and make things, so we figured it would be fun," Jessie said.

Violet was studying the pile of party items covering the counter. "We forgot to buy candles," she said. "You can't have a birthday party without candles for the cake!"

"I'll run back and get some," said Henry, turning away from the counter. As he headed down the paper goods aisle, he noticed a man and woman standing off to one side, whispering to each other. The woman was wearing a long fur coat and lots of fancy jewelry. Henry saw the man shake his head angrily at the woman. They were looking toward the checkout counter at Violet, Benny, and Jessie. Henry wondered what they were talking about, and if it had anything to do with his family. He quickly found the birthday candles and brought them up to the counter.

The man and woman walked to the checkout counter, holding a package of paper plates. The woman was looking at the children as if she wanted to say something.

"Why don't you go ahead of us," Violet suggested. "You've just got one thing and we've got this whole basket of stuff."

"Thank you, that's very nice," the woman said. "Did I overhear you talking about a birthday party service?"

"Yes," said Jessie. "We've just started our own company."

"I'm Janet Woodruff, and this is my husband, Bob." She motioned to the man next to her, who barely glanced at the children. He looked tired and unhappy. "My daughter, Sara, is having a party. What kinds of things do you do?" she asked.

"Whatever you and Sara would like," Jessie said. "We make decorations, bake the cake, and plan games for the kids."

"I was going to have that magician, Cassandra the Great," Mrs. Woodruff said, adjusting her heavy gold watch as she spoke. "But I think you kids would be better. And then I wouldn't have to deal with her manager, who seems to be an unpleasant character."

Bob Woodruff scowled. "At least the magician wouldn't make a big mess in our new house."

"We won't make a mess," said Benny. "We'll clean everything up."

Janet Woodruff gave her husband a quick glance, then turned to the children and said, "Why don't you give me your number and we can talk more about the party."

"Great," said Henry, jotting down their number on a scrap of paper and handing it to Mrs. Woodruff.

Janet Woodruff smiled and waved goodbye, her large diamond rings sparkling in the sunlight.

After they were gone, Henry said, "I saw them talking and looking at us, and I was wondering what they were saying."

"They must have been talking about hiring us," said Jessie.

"I guess so," said Henry. But he couldn't help wondering if there had been something more going on. He remembered how angry Mr. Woodruff had looked.

"Anyway, we'd better get going." Jessie turned to Ms. Fox, who was ringing up their items on the cash register. "We've got the party this Saturday afternoon for Alex Pierce and we need to go home and get ready for it."

"Is that the Pierces on Fieldstone Drive?" Ms. Fox asked. "The ones who live in that big mansion?"

"Yes, they do live on Fieldstone," Henry said.

The children noticed that Ms. Fox had stopped ringing up the items and was looking off into the distance as if thinking about something.

"Is something wrong?" Henry asked. "Are the Pierces friends of yours?"

Ms. Fox seemed startled. "No, oh, no . . . I don't know them." She finished adding up their purchases and put them into two large bags. When Jessie had paid, Ms. Fox handed the bags to Jessie and Henry.

"Have fun on Saturday," she called after them with a big smile.

"We will!" Benny called.

The Aldens walked a few stores down from Party Time to the grocery store. There they bought all the things they'd need to make the cake. Before they left, they stopped next to the store exit and put one of their posters up on the bulletin board.

"Now let's go home and get to work!" said Violet. She couldn't wait to begin making the decorations. She loved to paint and do all kinds of artwork.

"Hey, look who's over there!" said Benny. The Aldens turned to see the Woodruffs, pushing a cart through the produce section. Mrs. Woodruff was selecting oranges from a pile and putting them into their cart, but Mr. Woodruff was just standing idly beside her, his hands pushed into his pockets. When the Aldens waved, Mrs. Woodruff waved back. But Mr. Woodruff acted as if he didn't even see them.

The Aldens turned to go.

Benny said, "He doesn't seem very nice."

"Maybe something is bothering him," said Violet.

"I wonder what," Benny said.

"Probably something that's none of our business," said Jessie. "Come on, let's go home."

As they left the store, Henry turned around and saw Mr. Woodruff following his wife down an aisle, an unhappy look on his face.

The following Saturday, the Aldens arrived at the Pierces' house just after lunchtime, loaded down with supplies for the party. They brought the cake, which they'd baked the night before. They had cut and iced it to look just like a *Tyrannosaurus rex*, its eyes made of chocolate chips and its sharp, pointy claws and teeth made of candy corn.

"That's amazing," Mr. Pierce said when he saw the cake. "Alex will love it."

The Aldens immediately got to work in the basement, blowing up balloons, putting up streamers, and hanging up the dinosaur pictures they'd painted. In no time, the Pierces' basement was transformed into a jungle from millions of years ago.

"This is great!" Alex said when he came downstairs.

"You've really done a wonderful job," said Mrs. Pierce. "I feel like I've gone back in time — to the land of the dinosaurs!"

"We're glad you like it," said Jessie. "But now, Alex, you need to go upstairs so we can set up the dinosaur egg hunt."

"A dinosaur egg hunt! Wow!" said Alex. "Can't I stay and help?"

"It wouldn't be fair to the other kids if you knew where all the eggs were hidden," Henry pointed out.

"Oh, all right," Alex said as he followed his mother upstairs.

Jessie took out the bag of chocolate eggs, and she and Violet hid them around the room. Meanwhile, Henry and Benny hung up the Pin the Tail on the Dinosaur game they'd made. Then they set the table at the far end of the room.

The children had just finished setting everything up when the doorbell rang.

They heard Alex yell, "Hooray, they're

here!" Then they heard the sound of his feet pounding above them as he ran to the front door to greet his friends.

A few minutes later, Mrs. Pierce led a band of noisy boys and girls down to the basement.

Soon all the guests had arrived. Jessie gave them each a plastic bag and told them to start searching for "dinosaur" eggs.

When the eggs had all been found — and many of them eaten — the Aldens started a relay race. Several other games followed. Mr. and Mrs. Pierce stayed downstairs to watch, taking lots of pictures with their camera.

At last it was time for the cake. Jessie carried it over to Alex as everyone sang "Happy Birthday."

"Wow!" Alex said when he saw the *T rex* growling up at him from the cake platter.

"Don't forget to make a wish," Violet reminded him as he blew out the candles.

Everyone enjoyed the delicious cake filled with strawberry jam, whipped cream, and sliced fresh strawberries. Soon the doorbell was ringing again as parents arrived to pick up their children. As each child left, the Aldens gave him or her a small plastic dinosaur as a party favor.

At last all the kids had left.

"That was a great party!" said Alex.

"It sure was," his father agreed.

"I never realized how noisy ten kids could be," said Mrs. Pierce, collapsing onto the couch. "I'm glad you were here to help, because I never could have handled it!"

"And best of all, we'll do all the cleaning up now!" said Jessie.

As the Aldens began to clean up, the Pierces went upstairs.

The Aldens were almost done cleaning up when they heard a scream.

"What was that?" cried Violet.

"It sounded like Mrs. Pierce," said Henry as he and the other Aldens ran up the stairs.

They found Mrs. Pierce in the living room, a look of horror on her face. "We've been robbed!" she said.

CHAPTER 2

The Empty Safe

Mr. Pierce had just come down from the upstairs as the Aldens came up from the basement. "What's happened?" he said to his wife as he ran into the living room.

"We — we — we've been robbed," Mrs. Pierce repeated, and she started to cry.

"Calm down, dear," Mr. Pierce said, putting his arm around his wife. "Come sit down."

"I'll go get a tissue," Violet offered.

"That would be nice," Mr. Pierce said.

Then he sat down on the couch beside his wife. She was taking slow, deep breaths to calm herself.

Mr. Pierce waited until his wife had stopped crying. "Now tell me what happened," he said.

Mrs. Pierce sighed heavily and then began to speak. "I was just going to get some money to pay the Aldens." She motioned to the corner of the living room. "I went to the bank this morning and got cash. I took out a large sum because we are having that new dining room set delivered Monday morning and the store specifically asked for cash. I put it in the safe until the party was over. But when I went to open the safe just now, it was already open, and there was nothing inside."

Mr. Pierce got up and walked over to the corner of the room, where a small safe was built into a wooden cabinet. Just as his wife had said, the door of the safe hung open. It was empty.

"How much was in there?" Mr. Pierce asked.

"Several hundred dollars — some was for the Aldens and the rest was for the furniture," Mrs. Pierce said. "And now it's gone."

"I can't see how anyone could have stolen it — we've been home all day," said Mr. Pierce.

"Yes," said Henry. "But we were all down in the basement for the last few hours."

"And the kids were pretty noisy," Jessie added. "We never would have heard if someone had sneaked in."

"Do you really think someone would do that?" asked Mrs. Pierce, turning to her husband.

"It's possible," said Mr. Pierce.

"I just remembered," Mrs. Pierce added. "I unlocked the door when all the kids were arriving. I might have left it unlocked while we were downstairs."

"I've never seen a safe in someone's house before," Benny said.

"All the houses in this neighborhood were built by the same builder, and he put a safe in each living room," Mr. Pierce explained. "It's been very useful . . . until now."

"Would you like me to call the police for you?" asked Henry.

"Yes, thank you," Mr. Pierce said, gently patting his wife's back.

A few minutes later a police car arrived and an officer spoke to everyone about what they'd seen and heard that afternoon. Unfortunately, since they'd all been down in the basement enjoying the party, no one had much to tell her. When the officer was done with her questions, she promised to let the Pierces know as soon as she learned anything.

After the officer left, the Aldens finished cleaning up and headed home. Their joyful mood was gone.

"What a terrible thing to happen!" said Violet.

"I know," Jessie agreed. "I feel so bad for the Pierces."

"Well, at least the party went well," Henry pointed out.

"Yes, Alex and his friends did seem to have a good time," Jessie agreed.

"Maybe they'll catch the thief and everything will be okay," Violet said hopefully.

Jessie looked at her little brother and noticed that he was the only one who didn't seem sad. Instead, he had a thoughtful look on his face.

"What are you thinking about, Benny?" she asked him.

"I think this is another mystery for us to solve!" he said excitedly.

"Oh, Benny," Henry said, putting his arm around his brother. "I know you love mysteries. But let's leave this one for the police."

The next day, the phone rang just as the Aldens were sitting down to a big breakfast of pancakes and fresh fruit.

Henry answered. "Hello? Yes, this is Henry Alden," he said to the person on the other end. He listened for a moment and then said, "We're just about to have breakfast. We could come over right after that."

Jessie and Violet looked at each other questioningly. "I wonder who it is," said Jessie, carrying a big platter stacked with pancakes to the table.

Henry was looking at the calendar on the wall by the phone. "Two weeks from today sounds fine," he said into the telephone. "Nineteen Old Cedar Road. We'll be there in an hour." He hung up the phone and turned to his brother and sisters. "That was Mrs. Woodruff. She wants us to do her daughter's birthday party."

"That's great!" said Jessie, pleased that their business was taking off.

"Was she the one we met at Party Time?" Violet wanted to know.

"The one with the angry husband?" Benny added, his mouth full of pancakes.

"Yes, she's the one," Henry said.

"He must have changed his mind about us," said Jessie with a happy smile.

"I guess so," said Henry. But when he remembered how angry Mr. Woodruff had seemed at the grocery store, he thought that planning this party might turn out different from what they expected.

An hour later, the Aldens were sitting in the Woodruffs' living room, talking to Mrs.

Woodruff and six-year-old Sara. The house had been easy to find because it was just a block away from the Pierces' house.

"So what do you want to be when you grow up?" Jessie was saying to Sara.

"An astronaut!" Sara said excitedly. "We're learning about outer space in school, and I love it!"

"Maybe we could do an astronaut party," suggested Henry.

"What a wonderful idea," said Mrs. Woodruff.

"Yeah!" Sara agreed, her eyes glowing.

"The kids can all make their own astronaut helmets out of paper bags, and then we'll blast off to the moon," said Jessie.

"We can plan some games about rockets and space," Henry added.

"And we'll decorate the room with pictures of planets and stars," Violet said.

"Can I help you make the decorations? I'm really good at art," Sara said. "If I don't become an astronaut when I grow up, I'm going to be an artist."

"Sure, we'd love your help," Violet said.

The happy mood was interrupted when Mr. Woodruff came in, a tired, grim look on his face.

"Bob," Mrs. Woodruff said, her voice tense. "You remember the Aldens, don't you?"

Mr. Woodruff barely glanced at the children.

"They'll be doing Sara's birthday party," Mrs. Woodruff explained nervously.

"You know I'd rather just have that magician," said Mr. Woodruff.

"I think the Aldens will do a great job," said Mrs. Woodruff.

Sara mumbled something that no one could quite hear. She was looking at the floor and poking at the rug with her foot.

"What was that, dear?" Mrs. Woodruff asked.

Sara spoke a tiny bit louder. "I said, I wish Uncle John could be at my party."

Mrs. Woodruff said nothing. She just looked at her husband with concern.

Mr. Woodruff sighed deeply. "Well, he won't be here. You know that's not possible." And with that, he shuffled out.

For a moment, everyone just watched Mr. Woodruff go. Mrs. Woodruff tried to break the tension in the room. "Well, I guess you kids will want to go get started on the party planning," she said, trying to make her voice cheerful.

"Yes, first we'd better go buy supplies," Henry agreed. The Aldens stood up and began walking toward the door.

Violet couldn't help noticing how sad Sara looked. "Sara, would you like to come help us?" she asked.

Sara looked up eagerly. "Really? Could I?"

"Sure," Jessie said, smiling broadly. Then she turned to Mrs. Woodruff. "If that's okay with you, of course."

Sara looked hopefully at her mother.

"Sure, that sounds wonderful," said Mrs. Woodruff, glad the Aldens had thought of a way to cheer up her daughter.

As the Aldens walked toward the stores at the center of Greenfield, Violet and Sara walked a little bit behind the others.

"Was your uncle John very special to you?" Violet asked gently.

"Yes," Sara said quietly.

"It's hard when you lose someone you love," Violet said. The Aldens had lost their parents, and so they knew this better than most people.

"I don't think I want to talk about it," said Sara.

"I understand," Violet said. "But if you change your mind, I'm a good listener."

Sara smiled. "Thank you," she said.

Jessie and Benny had been walking ahead of the others. Just then Jessie stopped in her tracks. "Hey, what's going on?" she said angrily. Jessie was standing and staring at the GREENFIELD NEWS bulletin board.

"Remember we put a poster up here? It's gone!" Jessie said.

"Here's what's left of it." Henry pulled a shred of paper off the board. "Here's the picture of balloons that was up in the corner."

"Now there's just a big ad for Cassandra the Great," said Benny.

"What are you guys talking about?" asked Sara.

"Last week we put up posters advertising our birthday party service, and it looks like someone tore this one down," Jessie explained.

"That's too bad," said Sara. "I wonder why someone would tear down your poster."

No one could think why someone would do such a mean thing. As they continued on their way, Benny stopped to tie his shoe. The others went on ahead of him, knowing he'd quickly catch up.

When Benny stood up, he noticed a man in a long dark coat standing at the end of the street. He seemed to be watching Benny. But the sun was in Benny's eyes, and before Benny could figure out who the man was, he quickly stepped behind a tree.

There was something strange about how the man had stood so still, just staring. And there was something familiar about him. Benny began walking again.

After a few moments Benny looked back

Town
Council
Meeting

CASSANDRA
THE GREAT
GREENFIELDS
FAVORITE
MAGICIAN

over his shoulder and was surprised to see that the man was following him. Benny noticed that he was limping, as if he'd injured his right leg. When the man saw Benny look in his direction, he stopped walking and began to study the house he had been passing. But Benny didn't think the man was interested in the house at all.

Suddenly Benny began to feel a little nervous. Who was that man? And why was he following them?

Benny looked for his sisters and brother, but they were all far ahead of him by now.

Suddenly Benny felt very alone. "Wait for me!" he called, and he ran to catch up.

Meanwhile, the other Aldens were half a block ahead of Benny, looking for the other posters they'd put up around the town.

"Remember we had one there?" Jessie said, pointing to the hardware store window. "It's gone."

"And the one we put up in the deli is gone, too!" Violet said, pointing.

"Now both those windows have ads for

Cassandra the Great," said Henry.

"Do you think *she* tore down your posters and put up her own?" asked Sara.

"I'm beginning to wonder," said Jessie. "Cassandra entertains at birthday parties, too — maybe this is her way of getting rid of the competition."

"It isn't very nice," said Violet.

"Or maybe her manager did it," suggested Jessie. "Remember your mother said he was an unpleasant character."

"Well, we don't know for sure it was Cassandra," said Henry. "Maybe someone else took our posters down — maybe the store owners. She might just have put hers up afterward."

"Maybe," said Jessie.

Just then, Benny came running up, breathless and red-faced.

"Is something wrong?" Violet asked, when she saw how upset Benny looked.

"We're being followed!" Benny said.

CHAPTER 3

The Man with the Limp

Henry, Jessie, Violet, and Sara all looked back down the street to see who was following them. But the only people they saw were a young couple sitting on a bench and a mother pushing a stroller.

"Are you sure, Benny?" Henry asked.

"I don't see anyone now," Jessie pointed out.

Benny looked back down the street, also. "But — but — " Had he imagined that the man was following them? "There was a man behind us — I guess he's gone now."

"What did he look like?" Violet asked.

"I didn't really get a good look at him," Benny said. "But he was wearing a long dark coat. And he limped when he walked. And there was something about him. . . ." Benny paused.

"Something what?" Henry asked.

"I don't know," said Benny.

"Are you sure he was following us?" Jessie asked.

"Well, I guess I'm not *sure*. . . ." Benny admitted.

"We'll keep an eye out for him," said Henry. "In the meantime, let's go get our party supplies."

Soon the children were walking into Party Time. They were happy to see that at least no one had taken down their poster there.

"Hello, Aldens," Ms. Fox called when she saw them.

"Thanks for leaving up our poster," said Jessie. Then she told Ms. Fox what had happened to the other ones.

"Well, sometimes posters get ripped and

the store owners take them down so they won't look messy," Ms. Fox said. "I wouldn't worry about it. So, what are you in here for today?"

Sara eagerly told Ms. Fox all about her coming birthday and the party the Aldens were planning.

"That's exciting," said Ms. Fox. She turned to the Aldens. "Are Sara's parents the ones you met in here last week?"

"Yes, they are. Do you remember them?" Violet asked.

"I do," said Ms. Fox.

"It's a good thing they overheard us talking to you about our party service!" said Henry.

"Yes, it is, isn't it?" Ms. Fox said with a smile.

"We'd better get started," Jessie said, heading down the aisle that held art supplies.

The Aldens picked out paper and paints to make posters of the planets, and they found paper plates, napkins, and a tablecloth decorated with stars and moons.

"These are perfect!" said Sara.

For party favors, the Aldens chose little puzzles with pictures of rockets on them.

"I think we're all set now," said Jessie.

"Just don't forget the birthday candles!" Violet called out, and they all laughed.

The following afternoon, the Aldens met at Sara's house to work on the decorations. Violet traced the shapes of planets, comets, and moons on several pieces of paper, and the others painted them. Saturn was the most fun to paint, with its beautiful rings. After they'd been working for a while, Sara and Benny began to get restless.

"How about if we take a break now and go to the playground down the road?" Jessie suggested. "We can finish these later."

"Hooray!" said Benny as they rinsed their brushes and put the tops back on the paints.

In no time, the children were walking down the road. Sara had brought along a ball so they could play soccer on the field next to the playground. "Violet!" Sara called, kicking the ball down the wide sidewalk to the older girl.

Violet stopped the ball with her foot and passed it to Henry. Henry then kicked the ball to Benny.

Benny tried to stop Henry's pass, but the ball rolled off his foot and back down the sidewalk away from him. "I'll get it," Benny called over his shoulder as he ran back for the ball. He bent down to get it, and as he stood back up, he saw the man in the dark coat who'd been following them the day before. He was walking about half a block behind Benny, limping, just as Benny had noticed the day before.

But now the sun wasn't in his eyes, and Benny immediately recognized the man. "Mr. Woodruff!" he said under his breath. He started to say hello. But before he could, Mr. Woodruff turned and went behind a truck.

"That's strange," Benny said to himself. If it had been someone else, Benny would have gone after him and said hello. But he

was a little frightened of grouchy Mr. Woodruff.

So instead, Benny ran ahead to tell the others. But as he got closer, he began to feel funny. How could he tell Sara that her father was snooping around after them? He decided to tell Jessie or Henry and let them figure out what to do.

When Benny reached the playground, Violet and Sara were climbing on the monkey bars, and Jessie and Henry were sitting on the swings. Benny went straight over to the older children and told them whom he'd seen.

"That's strange," Jessie said. The children looked back down the road, but now there was nobody there.

"Where do you think he is now?" asked Henry.

"I don't know. Maybe hiding behind a tree or bush or something," said Benny. "But he was definitely following us."

"And you're sure it was Mr. Woodruff?" Henry said.

"Yes," Benny said.

"Why would he be following us?" Henry asked.

"Two days in a row!" added Benny.

"Maybe he just wants to keep an eye on his daughter," Jessie suggested.

"Yes, but sneaking around behind her is kind of a strange way to do it, isn't it?" said Henry.

Just then Sara ran over with a big grin on her face and grabbed the ball away from Benny. "I thought we were going to play soccer!" She ran onto the field. "Come on!"

The others followed Sara. But before Benny began to play, he looked down the road and around the playground. There was no sign of Mr. Woodruff. Still, Benny wondered if he was hidden somewhere nearby, watching them.

That night, the Aldens had just finished a delicious dinner of crispy fried chicken, creamy mashed potatoes, and buttery biscuits when the phone rang. Mrs. McGregor answered it. She was the family's housekeeper and the one who had made the wonderful meal. "Yes, they're right here," they heard her say. "Hold on just a minute — I'll put Jessie on."

Jessie took the call and talked for a moment before hanging up. "We've got another job!" she told the others excitedly.

"Really?" said Violet.

"That was a man named Mr. Grayson. He lives in the same neighborhood as the Pierces and the Woodruffs. In fact, it was Mrs. Woodruff who told him about us. He's planning his daughter Hallie's birthday party. It's this Saturday, and he needs us to help him."

"This Saturday! A rush job. I wish he'd called sooner," Henry said.

Jessie explained, "Mr. Grayson said they were going to have a skating party, and they rented the party room at the rink to serve the cake in. But now Hallie's broken her ankle. So they obviously can't have a skating party anymore. But he still wants to use the party room because he doesn't want kids running all over his house. He said he has a lot of fancy artwork and stuff there."

"We could plan some sitting-down games that they could play in the party room," Henry pointed out.

"That's just what I had in mind," said Jessie. "I told him we'd come up with some ideas and meet with them tomorrow afternoon."

"Sounds great," said Violet.

The children spent the evening thinking of ideas for Hallie's party. Since she'd wanted to have a skating party, they tried to keep the theme of winter sports. At last they'd come up with a bunch of fun games and interesting crafts for the kids to make.

"I think Hallie and her father will like these ideas," said Henry.

The following afternoon, the Aldens arrived at the Graysons' house. Mr. Grayson, a tall, thin man with a mustache, welcomed them into the living room.

"I can see why you don't want to have the party here," Jessie said, admiring all the beautiful sculptures and crystal vases on the tables and shelves.

"Yes, I'm an art collector and I have a lot

of valuable pieces here," Mr. Grayson said. "I couldn't take the chance that something would get broken."

Mr. Grayson motioned for the Aldens to sit down. "Sorry to call you on such short notice, but Hallie just broke her ankle. I happened to be chatting with Janet and Bob Woodruff, who are good friends of mine, and I told them my problem — fifteen guests invited for a party this Saturday, and no plans for entertaining them! Janet told me that you were planning Sara's party and had some wonderful ideas. In fact, she just couldn't say enough good things about you. So I figured I'd see if you could help us."

"We're glad you did," said Jessie.

Just then a girl about Violet's age hobbled into the room on crutches. She had a large cast on her ankle and looked very sad.

"This is my daughter, Hallie," Mr. Grayson said.

"Hello!" said Henry.

"Too bad about your ankle," Jessie added.

"Yeah," said Hallie, looking at the ground. "Now my birthday will be ruined."

"Wait until you hear the ideas we have," Benny piped up. "You'll *still* have a great birthday!"

Mr. Grayson couldn't help but smile at Benny's enthusiasm. But Hallie just slumped into a chair. She didn't even look at the Aldens.

Henry began talking. "We figured that since you wanted to have a skating party, you must like winter sports. So we've planned a puppet show and a lot of sitting-down games and crafts that are about winter."

"At least that's better than what my dad suggested," Hallie grumbled. "He wanted to have that magician. But we did that last year. I don't want to have the same party again."

Jessie wondered if Hallie was referring to Cassandra the Great, but she didn't ask. Instead she began to tell the Graysons about their ideas. "Do you and your friends like to make things?" she asked Hallie.

"Yeah, why?" Hallie said.

"You can each make your own snow

globe," Jessie said. "You make a little scene out of clay, put it in a small glass jar, and add water and some glitter for the snow." The night before, the Aldens had made a snow globe to show Hallie. Jessie pulled it out of her backpack.

For the first time since they'd met her, Hallie smiled. "Wow," she said, taking the homemade snow globe from Jessie and turning it around in her hands. She watched as the glittery "snow" floated down on the little log cabin scene Violet had created inside. "We can make these ourselves?"

"You sure can," said Violet. "It's easy. We'll bring all the supplies and show everyone what to do. Our neighbor has a baby, so we'll ask her for her empty baby food jars to make them in."

The Aldens then told her about a game they'd made up called "Melt the Ice Cube." It was a little like "Hot Potato." The kids would sit in a circle passing the "ice cube" — which was really a present wrapped in lots of layers of paper — in time to music. Each time the music stopped, whoever was holding the gift got to unwrap a layer. The one who tore off the last layer of wrapping paper got to keep the gift as a prize.

"That sounds like fun!" said Hallie. "And I can do it even with this stupid broken ankle!"

"You sure can," said Violet.

"Hey, tell her about the popcorn snowmen," said Benny.

"Popcorn snowmen?" asked Hallie.

"As a special treat to eat, all the kids can make their own popcorn snowmen," said Henry. "We'll start them before the party, by mixing popcorn and melted marshmallows, and rolling the mixture into balls. Then everyone can stack the popcorn balls and decorate them with candy to make them look like snowmen."

"And then you get to eat them!" Benny added.

Mr. Grayson smiled broadly. "It sounds like you kids have put a lot of thought into this party and come up with some great ideas — on very short notice!"

He was interrupted by the sound of the

phone ringing. "Excuse me," he said, picking up the receiver.

Hallie and the Aldens talked quietly while Mr. Grayson was on the phone. She was very excited about her birthday party now that she'd heard their wonderful ideas. Benny asked Hallie about the writing he saw on her cast. Hallie explained that her friends had written little get-well messages there. Then she pulled out some colored markers, and each of the Aldens signed her cast and drew pictures, too.

As they were working, Jessie looked over at Mr. Grayson, who was still on the phone. His face was red and he looked angry. His voice sounded tense.

She looked back at her drawing and tried to focus on it. But all of a sudden Jessie overheard Mr. Grayson say, "I'm sorry if you're angry, but I've already hired the Alden kids. I don't want to discuss this anymore." And he quickly hung up the phone.

CHAPTER 4

A Mysterious Phone Call

All the children looked over when they heard the receiver bang down.

"Who was that, Dad?" asked Hallie.

"Oh, nobody," Mr. Grayson said.

"You sounded upset," Hallie said.

"We'll talk about it later," Mr. Grayson answered.

Jessie knew it was none of her business. Still, she wondered what had made Mr. Grayson so angry.

"It wasn't that magic lady again, was it?" said Hallie.

"Magic lady?" her father said. "Oh, you mean the magician. Yes, as a matter of fact, it was." He turned to the Aldens and explained. "When Hallie broke her ankle, I knew the skating party was out. So I quickly called the same magician we'd had last year. She changed her plans to fit us in at the last minute. But Hallie wasn't too excited about having the same party she'd had last year.

"Then Janet Woodruff told me about you kids, so I canceled the magician. She and her manager are pretty angry now. Anyway . . ." Mr. Grayson seemed eager to change the subject. Looking down at Hallie's leg, he said, "What great drawings you made on Hallie's cast!"

"Doesn't it look nice now?" Hallie asked.

"We'd better get going — we've got to go to the party store and buy supplies," Jessie said.

"Great. Call and let me know how things are going," said Mr. Grayson.

"See you this weekend!" Hallie called as the Aldens left.

*   *   *

On their way to the store, the Aldens talked about what had just happened at the Graysons'.

"Do you think Mr. Grayson was talking on the phone to Cassandra the Great?" asked Violet.

"He might have been," said Jessie. "There aren't that many magicians in town who entertain at birthday parties. And he said it was a woman."

"If it was Cassandra and she was really angry at us for taking one of her jobs, that might explain why she tore down our posters," said Benny.

"That's right," said Jessie. "Mr. Grayson said she'd rearranged her plans for him."

"I hate to think that someone is so angry at us," said Violet. "We're not trying to steal her business."

"No, we're not," Jessie agreed. "And even if we have gotten some of her jobs, that doesn't make it right to tear down our posters."

"I was wondering . . ." said Benny.

"What?" asked Henry.

"What if it isn't Cassandra who's tearing down the posters?" Benny said.

"Are you thinking of her manager?" Jessie asked.

"Well, maybe *he* is," Benny said.

"It sounds as if you have another person in mind," Violet said.

"Yes," Benny said. "Mr. Woodruff."

"Mr. Woodruff?" Jessie asked. "Why would he do something so rotten?"

"Whenever we see him, he's very rude to us," Benny said. "And we saw him following us. What if he just doesn't like us for some reason and he wants our business to fail?"

"I guess that's possible," Jessie said doubtfully.

"Well, we just have to keep doing the best we can at each party," said Violet. "Then our business is sure to be a success."

Soon they reached Party Time. When they entered the store, Ms. Fox gave them a cheery hello. "Are you kids back *again*?" she asked.

"We've just been hired to do another party!" Benny said excitedly.

"Wow, that business of yours is really taking off!" Ms. Fox said. "Whose party is it this time?"

Jessie told Ms. Fox about Hallie Grayson and her broken ankle.

"Poor kid," said Ms. Fox. "I remember I broke my ankle when I was a kid. It's hard being on crutches when you want to go out and play."

"She was planning to have a skating party, too," said Violet. "We're still going to celebrate at the rink, though. They have a special room for parties. The kids will play games and make things instead of skating."

"Why not just have the party at their house?" Ms. Fox asked.

"Their house has lots of fancy artwork, so her father doesn't want kids running around there," Henry explained.

"Well, I'm sure it will be great," said Ms. Fox.

"We'd better hurry up and get started," said Jessie. "The party is this Saturday afternoon!"

The Aldens picked out plates and napkins

with snowflakes on them. For decorations they bought sparkly silver tinsel to hang up like icicles. They bought colored felt and yarn for making puppets, and for the snow globes they bought colored quick-drying clay and glitter.

"And finally," said Jessie, "we'll get this little stuffed snowman as the prize for the Melt the Ice Cube game."

The children finished making their purchases and headed home to begin working.

The Aldens managed to get everything done by Saturday. It was a cold, crisp day when the Aldens arrived at the rink to begin setting up. They hung the tinsel and snowflakes they'd made, and covered the table with the pretty snowflake tablecloth.

"It looks great," Hallie said when she got there.

As soon as the guests arrived, Jessie and Violet taught all the kids how to make their own snow globes. Each girl or boy ended up making something quite different. One made a snowman and another a little teddy bear. Hallie made a girl ice-skating.

At the end of the party, when the clay was hard, the Aldens would put water and glitter into the jars to finish the snow globes.

The puppet show was a great success — the children shouted and laughed and threw confetti when they were supposed to.

When the party was almost over, the Aldens got the cake ready. They had baked it in the shape of a snowman, using three different-sized round cake pans for the body and head. They had iced the cake with white icing and shredded coconut to look like snow. The snowman's eyes, nose, and mouth were made from candy, the arms were pretzel sticks, and a piece of red licorice around its neck made a scarf.

Hallie's eyes lit up when she saw the cake. She turned to the Aldens and said, "This is the best birthday party ever! Thank you." Then she blew out the candles.

After the party favors had been given out, the guests had all gone home, and everything had been cleaned up, the Graysons and Aldens said good-bye.

"Thank you so much for everything," Hallie said as she gave each of the Aldens a hug. "You made this birthday really special. You really did a wonderful job. I'll recommend you to all my friends."

"That would be great," said Henry.

"Enjoy the rest of your day!" Jessie called as the Graysons drove off.

Grandfather had told the children he'd pick them up at four o'clock, a half hour after the party ended, so they'd have time to clean up. It was now ten minutes to four.

As the children waited for Grandfather, they heard the music playing from the ice-skating rink.

"I want to go skating!" Benny said.

"That's a great idea," said Jessie. "I'll call Grandfather and tell him not to pick us up until six."

The Aldens went back inside the rink. While Jessie found a phone, the others rented skates.

"Grandfather said that would be fine," Jessie said when she came back. She got a pair of skates for herself. The others had already laced up and were waiting for her.

Soon all four children were out on the ice, skating around in time to the music. Henry zoomed around quickly. Hockey was one of his favorite sports. Benny was still a little unsteady on his skates, so he just went slowly, trying not to fall. Violet tried the new moves her hockey coach had been teaching her — crossing her skates over and skating backward. Jessie went straight to the middle of the ice and practiced her graceful spins and turns.

Too soon it was quarter to six. The children returned their skates and put their shoes back on. When they got outside, Grandfather was just pulling up to the curb.

"How was the skating?" he asked when they'd all gotten inside the car and buckled their seat belts.

"It was great!" said Jessie.

"And the party went well?" Grandfather wanted to know.

"It did. Hallie was really pleased," Henry said.

As they drove, the children told their

grandfather about their afternoon. The ride home took them past the Graysons' house. As they turned onto Hallie's street, the children saw a police car parked right in front of the Graysons'.

"Look, a police car!" Benny cried.

The Aldens looked at the Graysons' house as they went by, but they could see nothing wrong from the outside.

As soon as they got home, Mrs. McGregor met them at the door, a concerned look on her face. "Henry, Mr. Grayson called a little while ago. He asked you to call him as soon as you got home."

"Thanks, Mrs. McGregor," Henry said, going straight to the phone.

He dialed and then waited a moment. "Hello, Mr. Grayson," he said when he heard the man pick up. "It's Henry Alden. Is everything okay?"

"Well," Mr. Grayson said, "the party was wonderful. But when we got home, we found we'd been robbed!"

CHAPTER 5

"I'll Get Rid of Them!"

"Oh, no!" Henry said. He sounded so upset that the rest of the family looked over to see what was the matter. "We'll be right over." He hung up the phone.

"What happened?" Jessie asked.

"You'll never believe it," Henry said. "The Graysons were robbed, too!"

For a moment everyone was silent. Then Violet said, "Just like the Pierces, during their party."

"Yes," said Henry.

"What's going on?" Benny asked.

"I don't know," said Henry, "but I told Mr. Grayson we'd be right over."

A few minutes later the Aldens arrived at the Graysons' house. The police car that had been parked in front of the house was gone now.

Mr. Grayson answered the door, looking grim. "Ah, the Aldens," he said. "Come in."

The Aldens followed Mr. Grayson into the living room, where Hallie was sitting looking very sad. Mr. Grayson motioned to the Aldens to sit down.

For a moment he didn't say anything. He just sat rubbing his forehead wearily.

"Mr. Grayson?" Grandfather said at last. "What happened?"

Mr. Grayson looked up at the Aldens, as if he'd forgotten they were there. Then he sighed and began speaking. "Hallie and I got back from the party at about four. As soon as we came in, something felt wrong. When I came in here, I immediately saw that the door to my safe was open. Some-one had broken into it and stolen all the valuables inside. They also took a few small — but expensive — works of art. It seems they took whatever they could carry with them."

"How terrible!" said Jessie.

"Do you have an alarm?" Henry asked.

"Yes, I do," said Mr. Grayson. "But I guess they knew how to cut the wires."

"They must have realized you were out and wouldn't be back for a while," Grandfather pointed out.

"I guess so . . ." Mr. Grayson agreed. And once again, he slumped over, holding his head in his hands.

"Don't worry, Mr. Grayson," Benny said. "We'll figure out who did this. We're good at solving mysteries."

Mr. Grayson looked up at Benny, and for the first time since the party, he smiled a small smile. "Thank you, Benny. That's good to know."

"But I don't think I can solve any mysteries right now," Benny said. "I'm too hungry to think!"

Everyone laughed.

Jessie looked at her watch. It was nearly seven o'clock. "Have you had any dinner yet?" she asked the Graysons.

"No," said Mr. Grayson. "I didn't realize it was that late."

"I am getting kind of hungry, Dad," Hallie said.

"You've had a terrible shock," Jessie said. "How about if we whip up a quick dinner for you."

"Yeah, eating always makes me feel better," said Benny.

"Oh, that's not necessary," Mr. Grayson said.

"Are you sure?" asked Henry. "We're good cooks."

"They are good cooks," said Grandfather, "and they would like to help."

"Party planners, mystery solvers, and cooks — is there anything you kids can't do?" Mr. Grayson said with a grin. "Come on in the kitchen and we'll see what we've got. But you must stay and have dinner with us."

The Aldens were glad to see that Mr.

Grayson was feeling a little better. Together they found a large box of spaghetti and a jar of tomato sauce in the pantry.

"We'll have a good dinner ready in no time," said Jessie. "Why don't you and Hallie and Grandfather just relax for a little while."

"If I were you, I'd want to play with my birthday presents," Benny said to Hallie.

A big smile appeared on Hallie's face. "Good idea, Benny," she said. "I'd almost forgotten it was my birthday."

While Mr. Grayson and Grandfather sat in the living room talking and Hallie played with all the wonderful gifts her friends had brought her, the Aldens got to work in the kitchen.

Violet found a loaf of Italian bread in the bread box and spread it with butter and sprinkled it with garlic. Then she wrapped it in tinfoil and put it in the oven.

While she was waiting for the water to boil for the spaghetti, Jessie put a pot of sauce on the stove. Then she and Benny set the table.

When Benny called the Graysons to come in for dinner, Mr. Grayson and Hallie were quite impressed with what they saw. Henry had piled each plate with a large serving of spaghetti and heaped steaming-hot sauce on top. He'd sprinkled each mound with freshly grated Parmesan cheese he'd found in the refrigerator. In the center of the table were a bowl of fresh crisp salad and a basket of warm, buttery garlic bread.

"This is a feast!" said Mr. Grayson.

"Everything looks delicious," Hallie agreed.

The Aldens and the Graysons sat down and enjoyed the meal. As they ate, they talked about lots of different things, but made sure not to talk about the burglary.

After dinner, Mr. Grayson and Hallie helped the Aldens clean up and wash the dishes.

"I guess we'd better get home now," Grandfather said when everything was put away.

"Let us know if you hear anything from the police," said Jessie.

"We certainly will," Mr. Grayson said. "And thank you again, for everything."

On their way home, the Aldens talked about the burglary. "Isn't it strange that we've done two parties, and each time the house was robbed?" said Henry.

"I'm sure it's just a coincidence," Grandfather said. "I read in the local paper that there have been several burglaries in Greenfield recently. I'm sure they have nothing to do with your parties."

"I guess not," said Henry. But he didn't sound convinced.

The next day the Aldens went to the Woodruffs' house to work on the outer space decorations for Sara's party. They headed straight down to the basement, where they'd left the pictures of planets they'd painted several days before. Since the paint was dry, Henry got to work cutting the planets out, as Violet traced stars and rocket ships for the others to paint.

"Oh, no," Violet muttered to herself.

"What's the matter?" Jessie asked.

"I just thought of something we forgot to buy," Violet said. "Glitter for the stars. I was going to mix it into the paint to make the stars sparkle."

"Don't we have some left from the snow globes?" Henry asked.

"No, we used it all up," Violet said.

"Why don't you all start painting the moons and rockets, and I'll walk into town and get some more glitter," Jessie suggested.

"I'll come with you," Benny offered.

Jessie and Benny put on their coats and walked to the store. At Party Time they walked straight to the arts and crafts aisle. Jessie picked out a large container of silvery glitter. She was just about to bring it up to the front of the store to pay for it when she overheard a man and a woman talking in the next aisle.

"Cassandra, you can't do that!" the man was saying.

"Oh, can't I?" a woman replied in a strong, confident voice. "If I don't do something soon, my whole birthday party business will be ruined. And you know as well as I do that it's a big part of my income."

"Benny!" Jessie whispered. "That might be Cassandra the Great in the next aisle."

Benny's eyes opened wide. "Do you really think so?"

"Shhh!" Jessie hushed him, so she could hear what the two were saying.

"I know lately things haven't been working out the way you'd like — " the man had been saying, but the woman named Cassandra cut him off.

"No, they haven't — and it's all because of them," she said angrily. "You do agree that they're the whole problem, don't you?"

"Yes, it does seem that way," the man agreed.

"If I can't get them to do what I want, then I'll just get rid of them," said Cassandra.

"You wouldn't do that, would you?" the man asked.

"Just watch me," said Cassandra.

Jessie and Benny heard quick, strong footsteps walking up the aisle. Then they heard the bell on the store's front door ring, and the store grew quiet. They knew that Cassandra and the man had left.

"Wow, what do you think they were talking about?" Benny asked Jessie.

"I don't know," Jessie replied. "But before we start trying to figure that out, let's find out if that really was Cassandra the Great."

"How many Cassandras could there be in Greenfield?" Benny asked.

"Probably only one, but I want to be sure," said Jessie.

The children brought the container of glitter up to the front of the store. Ms. Fox was behind the counter as usual. "More glitter?" she asked. "Didn't you just buy some of this a few days ago?"

"You have a good memory," Jessie said, getting the money out of her pocket to pay. "We were wondering, did you see that woman who just left?"

"Yes," said Patti Fox. "That's Cassandra the Great." She pointed to the poster on the wall. "You know, the magician. She and her manager come in every once in a while to buy supplies for her shows. Did you know she's doing a show right here at the community theater tomorrow night?" Other customers entered the store, and Ms. Fox turned to help them. "See you kids later!" she called.

The Aldens walked out of Party Time. "So that was Cassandra the Great and her manager," Jessie said. "Too bad we didn't get to see what they looked like."

"Ms. Fox said she's doing a show tomorrow night!" Benny said. "Can we go see it? I love magic."

Jessie was silent for a moment before she spoke. "You know, Benny, that's not such a bad idea. It will be fun. And I think it's about time we found out just who this Cassandra person is, and if she's trying to put us out of business. I'll call Grandfather from that pay phone on the corner. If he says it's okay, we can stop at the theater and buy tickets."

As the children walked to the phone, they talked about the conversation they'd overheard in Party Time.

"What do you think she was talking about?" Benny asked his sister. "She sounded pretty angry."

"Yes, she did," Jessie agreed. "She said that if she didn't do something soon, her birthday party business would be ruined. I wonder what that meant."

"Do you think she could have been talking about our taking some of her business?" Benny asked.

"Maybe. She also said, '*They're* the whole problem,'" Jessie reminded him.

"You mean, 'they' might be *us*?" Benny asked.

"Maybe," Jessie said.

"But Jessie, don't you remember what else she said?" Benny asked, his voice becoming anxious. "She said, 'If I can't get them to do what I want, then I'll just get rid of them'!"

Jessie and Benny both stopped walking and stared at each other.

CHAPTER 6

Mr. Woodruff's Workshop

When Jessie and Benny got back to the Woodruffs' house, they wanted to tell the others what had happened in town. But Sara was there, and they decided to wait until they were alone.

All the decorations were done except the stars. The children quickly mixed the glitter with the yellow paint and painted the stars.

As they were working, Mr. Woodruff came downstairs, as grouchy as ever.

"Are you kids here again?" he asked.

"We've got a lot to do if we want this party to be really great," Henry explained.

Mr. Woodruff walked slowly around the basement, looking at all the decorations the children had painted. He was frowning the whole time. The children waited anxiously, wondering what he would say about them. But he said nothing. Instead he noticed some spots on the linoleum floor. "You spilled some paint here," he said, annoyed.

"Don't worry, Mr. Woodruff. It's washable paint," said Henry quickly. "We'll clean everything up before we go."

"Make sure you do," Mr. Woodruff grumbled. "There are cleaning supplies in there." He motioned to a door. "And Sara, have you cleaned your room yet?"

"No, Dad," Sara said quietly. "I was going to do it later."

"You'd better have it done before dinnertime," her father said before heading upstairs.

Benny was sitting silently. He had a thoughtful look on his face.

Sara was also sitting quietly, her face red. At last she spoke softly. "I'm sorry about my dad. He's not usually like this. It's been a hard year. Ever since Uncle John . . ." She stopped, and said nothing more.

"That's okay," Violet said. "Sometimes people act differently when they're feeling sad or something is bothering them."

"Yes, I guess so," Sara muttered.

Henry opened the door Mr. Woodruff had indicated, looking for a sponge. The door led into a large workshop. There were some large pieces of machinery and some long wooden boards propped up in a corner. The floor was covered with sawdust.

Sara followed him in. "This is my dad's workshop," she explained.

"Looks like he's good with his hands," Henry said, impressed by all the tools. "What kind of things does he make?"

"He doesn't make things as much as fix things," Sara said. "You know, anything that breaks — my mom's radio, my Rollerblades. Once he even had to fix the lock on our safe when it got stuck."

"The lock on your safe?" Henry repeated.

"Yeah, we have a safe built into a cabinet in our living room," Sara said. "My parents keep jewelry in there, you know, expensive stuff like that."

Henry nodded quietly, but his mind was racing. He'd had no idea that Mr. Woodruff was good at fixing things — like locks on safes. Could he be the one who'd been breaking into safes? He'd have to discuss this with the others on their way home.

Sara and Henry found cleaning supplies in a corner cabinet. They returned to the main part of the basement and wiped up the drips of paint. Violet was setting out the last few painted stars to dry.

"Well, we're all done here. We'd better get going. We promised Mrs. McGregor we would help her with chores today," said Jessie.

"And she's making macaroni and cheese tonight!" Benny said excitedly.

"You wouldn't want to miss that," Sara said with a smile.

*   *   *

On the way home, Jessie said, "Wait until you hear what Benny and I overheard today at Party Time," and she told them the whole story of Cassandra's angry words and of the magic show she had gotten tickets for.

"Cassandra the Great?" Henry asked.

"The one and only!" Jessie said. "She's doing the show tomorrow night at the community theater. I thought we should see who our competition is!"

"Do you really think Cassandra was talking about us in Party Time?" Violet asked.

"I don't know," said Jessie. "It's possible. Right, Benny?"

But Benny didn't answer. He hadn't been listening.

"Benny, what's the matter?" Jessie asked. "Is something bothering you?"

"I was just thinking about when Mr. Woodruff came down to the basement," Benny said. "Did anyone notice how he was walking?"

"Was there something odd about the way he walked?" Henry asked.

"No," Benny said.

Now the others were really confused.

"Benny, what are you talking about?" Jessie demanded.

"Don't you see?" said Benny. "He walked like everybody else. Mr. Woodruff didn't have a limp!" Benny said.

"Oh," Jessie said, understanding at last. "But when you saw him following us, he was limping."

"Yes," said Benny. "I just don't get it."

"Maybe he only limps when he walks a long way," Jessie said. "Or maybe he had pulled a muscle and now it's healed."

"Yes, or maybe it wasn't really Mr. Woodruff you saw," Violet suggested.

"But I was sure it was," Benny said, looking confused. "Now I don't know what to think!"

"Well, listen to this," Henry said. He told the others what Sara had told him about her father fixing the lock on a safe. And then he added, "If he can fix a lock, he probably knows how to break into one."

CHAPTER 7

The Magic Show

"I can't find my new shoes!" Benny called.

"Can someone tie my purple hair ribbon?" Violet asked.

It was the following night and the Aldens were getting ready to go to the magic show. They were all getting dressed up in their best clothes. The boys were in slacks and jackets, and the girls wore pretty dresses. Even Grandfather was wearing a suit and his red flannel vest.

"Here are your shoes," Henry said,

pulling them out from under Benny's bed.

"Oh, is that where they were," said Benny. "How did you know?"

"Because that's where I always find them when you forget to put them away in the closet, silly," Henry said.

Meanwhile, Jessie was tying a purple satin ribbon in Violet's hair. "There," Jessie said, standing back and looking at her work. "You look very pretty, and the bow matches your dress perfectly."

"Thanks," Violet told her sister. "And you look nice, too."

In a short while the Aldens arrived at the community theater. A large crowd filed into the auditorium. There were lots of young children, and the air was filled with the buzz of excited voices.

Jessie heard a boy next to her say, "This is the same magician that I saw at Billy's birthday party. She was great!"

A man in front of them was telling another man, "Yes, we saw her here last year. She puts on a great show."

As soon as the lights began to dim, the

voices hushed. Music played and the lights came up on the stage. Then Cassandra appeared, dressed magnificently in a purple satin dress with a matching top hat and cape. The audience broke into applause.

Cassandra was a tall woman with long, flowing brown hair. She walked gracefully back and forth across the stage, smiling out at the audience and bowing her head slightly in thanks for the applause. As soon as she spoke, Jessie and Benny recognized the voice they'd heard in Party Time. Only now she didn't sound angry. Now her voice was calm and cool.

Cassandra began with some small tricks, pulling silk flowers and scarves from her cape and hat. She heaped the colorful scarves and flowers on a small round table to her right. She juggled some sparkly balls and made them disappear. She poured a glass of milk into her hat, and the milk vanished. With each trick she invited the audience to help her by repeating the magic words she recited. The Aldens eagerly joined in, laughing and clapping at the tricks.

The next trick was a card trick. A girl Cassandra had chosen from the audience had to pick cards from a deck and Cassandra guessed the numbers. Amazingly, she was right every time. After the girl sat down, Cassandra called up another volunteer — this time a boy sitting near the stage.

Cassandra asked the boy to write his name and favorite ice cream flavor on a piece of paper. She took the paper from him.

Everyone was very surprised by what she did next. She tore up the paper into little pieces and dropped them into her hat. Then she waved her hand over the hat and pulled out — a whole sheet of paper. The paper wasn't even crumpled. When Cassandra turned the hat upside down, there was nothing else inside — no torn scraps. Next Cassandra held up the paper and read from it. "Mint chocolate chip," she said. "Is that your favorite kind of ice cream?"

The boy nodded.

"And your name is Kevin?" Cassandra asked.

"Yes," said Kevin, obviously amazed. "But you just tore up what I wrote. How did you . . . ?"

"That's my secret," Cassandra said, sending Kevin back down to his seat. "And now we're going to take a short break. But make sure you're back in your seats for the second half of the show!" The audience began clapping, and Cassandra smiled and curtsied before the curtain fell.

"That was great!" Benny said as the lights came back on.

"It sure was," Henry agreed.

"She seems so nice," said Violet. "It's hard to believe she said all those mean things and might be trying to run us out of business."

"You're right," said Jessie. "She doesn't sound anything like she did yesterday at Party Time."

"How about some Cokes?" Grandfather suggested. They all walked out to the lobby and enjoyed drinks and popcorn before returning to their seats.

The second half was even more exciting than the first. Cassandra was now wearing a sparkly red outfit with a matching red top hat. She took a live dove from her top hat and placed both dove and hat on the little round table, where the dove settled comfortably on the brim of the top hat among the silk scarves and flowers. Then she blew up some long thin balloons and twisted them into animal shapes — a dog, a bird, a monkey in a tree. She threw the first two balloon animals to eager children in the audience. But the monkey she put under her cape — and when she lifted her cape, it was gone. She did several more tricks and then paused and spoke dramatically. "I need three volunteers for my last and most amazing trick," Cassandra said.

"Pick me, pick me!" Benny whispered under his breath as he reached his arm up as high as he could.

"You in the blue jacket," Cassandra said, pointing right at Benny, "and the girls on either side of you."

Benny, Jessie, and Violet turned around to make sure she was really pointing at them. "Us?" Benny asked.

"Yes," Cassandra said with a smile, "you three."

"Go on!" Henry said, patting each of them on the back as they slid down the row of seats and walked up the aisle to the stage.

"What are your names?" Cassandra asked Benny.

They each said their names in turn.

Cassandra seemed surprised. She paused for a minute. "Did you say *Alden*?" she asked.

"Yes," Benny said.

Then Cassandra recovered from her surprise. "Well, do you see this big box behind us that's covered by a cloth?"

"Yes," they answered.

"Benny, Violet, go pull the cloth off," Cassandra said.

They did as they were told. Underneath the cloth was no ordinary box. It was a safe.

"This trick is called the Mystery of the Empty Safe," Cassandra said. "Jessie, will you hand me what's inside the safe?" Jessie opened the door to the safe, which was not locked. Inside was a large bag with a dollar sign on the front. She lifted out the bag and gave it to Cassandra. It was quite heavy.

"What's inside?" Cassandra asked, holding out the bag so Jessie could put her hand in.

Jessie reached in and pulled out some gold coins. "Looks like gold," she said.

"Ah, money," Cassandra said, her eyes lighting up. "Now, Violet and Benny, look inside the safe and tell me if you see anything else."

"No," Benny said after he'd looked.

"Just an empty safe," said Violet.

"Now, all of you, feel the safe — try to move it. Is it heavy? Does it feel solid, like a real safe?" Cassandra asked.

Benny, Jessie, and Violet banged on the safe with their hands, tried to push it, and walked all around it, inspecting it closely.

"It feels very solid," said Jessie.

"Put the money bag back inside, please, Jessie," Cassandra instructed.

Again Jessie did as she asked. Then Cassandra shut the door of the safe and turned the lock on the front. "Now, each of you see if you can open the safe."

Benny, Jessie, and Violet each tried pulling the door open, but it was locked shut. Benny even tried turning the lock, but the door still wouldn't open.

"I bet I can open it," Cassandra said. She stepped in front of Benny and waved her hand over the safe. Then she knocked two times on the top of the safe, stepped back, and the door swung open by itself. Inside, the safe was empty.

The audience gasped and then began applauding. Jessie, Violet, and Benny smiled in surprise. Cassandra bowed deeply, and then showed the Alden children off the stage. Cassandra bowed one more time, the curtain fell, and the show was over.

Grandfather was standing up, putting on his coat and wrapping his scarf around his throat, when he noticed that none of his grandchildren were ready to go. They were

all staring at the curtained stage, looking amazed and confused.

"Can you believe that last trick she did?" Jessie said at last.

"Wasn't that wonderful?" said James Alden. "I'll never guess how she did it."

"That's not what Jessie means," Henry said. "That trick was . . . well, it's exactly what's happened to the two families we've given parties for. At the end of the parties their safes are empty."

"Well, isn't that a funny coincidence," Grandfather said.

"If it *is* just a coincidence," Henry said.

"What do you mean?" their grandfather asked.

"I think we'd better tell you about this in the car," Jessie said. She and the others quickly put on their coats, hats, and mittens. Once they were in the car, Jessie told Grandfather about their torn posters, which had been replaced by Cassandra's posters, and about the angry phone call Cassandra had made to Mr. Grayson. They also told him about the conversation they'd overheard in Party Time. "We've been wondering if we're the ones she was talking about — if she's mad at us for taking away some of her birthday party business. We're afraid she's trying to get rid of us — or at least our party business. And now that empty safe trick really makes me wonder. . . ."

"You don't think she robbed those two families, do you?" Grandfather asked.

"I can't believe she'd really do that," said Henry. "And yet . . ."

"She's such a successful magician," Mr. Alden said. "Why would she risk committing crimes to make money, when she does so well with her magic shows?"

"Yes, but not with her birthday party business, and she said that was a big part of her income. Anyway, maybe she didn't rob the safes for the money," Jessie offered. "Maybe she just did it as a prank, because she was mad at the families that used us for their parties."

"That's a pretty dangerous prank," Henry said.

"Yes, it is," Jessie agreed.

"I noticed something else," said Violet, who'd been quiet since the show ended. "Remember when we went up on stage and Cassandra asked our names? Did anyone notice something strange about her reaction?"

"Yes, I'd forgotten, but I did notice that," said Benny. "When we told her, she looked surprised. She said, 'Did you say *Alden*?' as if she'd heard our name before."

"That would make sense if she knows about our birthday party service," said Jessie.

"Maybe Cassandra isn't to blame at all," said Henry. "Maybe it's her manager using her party service as a cover for his own burglaries."

"You kids and your mysteries," said Grandfather. "I agree that there have been some strange coincidences happening lately, but I hope you're not going to jump to any conclusions about Cassandra."

"Don't worry, Grandfather, we won't," Henry assured him. "But we're not going to rest until we've solved this."

CHAPTER 8

The Watcher in the Woods

That weekend was Sara's birthday party. The day before, the Aldens went to her house to bake the cake and put together the last of the games. Sara had wanted to help and her mother offered their big kitchen.

"So what kind of cake do you want?" Jessie asked Sara.

"Chocolate!" Sara said without pausing for a moment. "A chocolate cake with chocolate frosting."

"That's a lot of chocolate!" said Benny.

But he was excited because he loved chocolate, too.

Henry came up with the idea of making the cake in the shape of a rocket ship. "We'll decorate it with candy and marshmallows to look like a real rocket."

"And remember those little plastic astronauts we bought at Party Time?" Violet recalled. "We can attach some of those to the cake with long strings of licorice, so it looks like they're floating outside the spaceship."

Jessie had borrowed a cookbook from Mrs. McGregor, and Benny searched the dessert section for a good recipe.

"Use this one. Mrs. McGregor has made it a lot of times," Benny commented.

"How can you tell?" Sara wondered.

"Look at all the grease spots and chocolate stains on this page," he said, pointing.

Everyone laughed. "You're right, Benny. This is probably the chocolate cake she always makes for Grandfather's birthday," said Henry. "It's great!"

Jessie wrote the ingredients down on a small sheet of paper and stuffed it into her pocket. Then the children all set off for the grocery store.

After they bought everything they needed, Sara and the Aldens returned to Sara's house and got to work. They went straight to the kitchen, where they unloaded all the groceries and put on aprons.

While the cake was baking, the children made the chocolate icing by beating together butter, powdered sugar, and melted chocolate. Then they cleaned up, putting away all the unused supplies, washing the bowls and measuring spoons and cups, and wiping the counters with a sponge.

Ding! At last the timer went off, telling them the cake was ready.

After the cake had cooled, Henry carefully cut it in the shape of a rocket. Benny and Sara eagerly gobbled up the extra bits. "Yum! This is almost as good as when Mrs. McGregor makes it!" said Benny.

While Benny and Sara were licking their chocolaty fingers, the older children frosted the cake and decorated it.

"Wow!" said Sara when she saw what they'd done. "I love it!"

"Now we'd better finish making the games," said Jessie.

"What's left to do?" asked Sara.

"Remember that big box we brought over here the other day?" Jessie asked. "We've got to turn that into a rocket for you and your friends to ride in."

"How are we going to do that?" Sara asked.

"You'll see," said Violet.

Sara led the way out to the garage, where they'd stored the large box.

"It's such a beautiful day, we can work on it outside in your driveway," Jessie suggested.

"That way we won't have to worry about dripping paint and making my father mad!" Sara said.

The box had held a large television set, so it was big enough for two children to sit inside. Jessie and Henry cut large windows on the sides of the box and covered them with black paper. Then they decorated the outside of the box with an American flag and made panels of buttons and knobs and dials and switches on the inside.

They'd been working for a while when Jessie noticed that Violet wasn't helping. She was just looking off into the woods beyond Sara's house.

"What's wrong?" Jessie asked her sister.

Violet didn't answer.

"Violet?" Jessie said again.

"Oh!" Violet seemed startled. She looked around at the other children, who were all hard at work on the rocket ship. She motioned to Jessie, and the two girls moved a little bit away from the rest of the group. Then Violet began speaking quietly. "I saw someone in the woods out there watching us. A man. I saw him a few times — but it seemed as if every time I'd get a good look at him he'd see me and hide. Then he'd show up in a different spot."

"Was it Mr. Woodruff?" Jessie asked.

Violet thought for a moment. "It might have been. It's so dark in those trees that it was hard to tell for sure."

"Or maybe it was Cassandra's manager,"

Jessie suggested. "I don't know what he looks like — I only know his voice, from the party store."

The two girls were quiet for a few minutes as they looked out at the woods to see if anyone was there.

"He seems to be gone now," said Violet.

"That reminds me of something I wanted to ask Sara," Jessie said, moving back over to where the other kids were.

"Sara," she said, "Benny said he saw your dad limping the other day. Did he hurt his leg?"

Sara looked confused. "No. I've never seen my dad limp."

The Aldens all looked at one another.

"Are you sure?" Jessie asked. "Maybe he'd pulled a muscle or something."

"No," said Sara. "Not that I know of."

"Well, never mind," Jessie said.

Sara and the Aldens finished painting and decorating the rocket ship. When at last they were done, they slipped inside two at a time to see how it felt to "fly" the ship.

"My friends are going to love this!" Sara said.

When they got home from Sara's a short while later, they gathered in the old boxcar in the backyard. Violet told the others about the man she'd seen watching them.

"That's pretty strange," said Henry.

"But isn't it even stranger that Sara said her father doesn't have a limp — and never did?" said Benny.

"It sure is," said Jessie.

"I've been worrying about something else," Henry said. "We've done two parties, and during both there was a burglary. What if it happens again tomorrow?"

"I thought of that, too," said Jessie. "Whoever's doing the burglaries seems to know when we've got a party scheduled."

"Cassandra knew about Hallie's party," Violet recalled. "Mr. Grayson said he'd canceled her when he heard about us."

"I wonder if she knew about Alex's party," said Henry.

"Only one way to find out," said Jessie. "Let's call and ask."

The children went into the house, and Jessie led the way to the family room. There, she picked up the phone and dialed the Pierces' number. A moment later she said, "Hello, Mrs. Pierce, it's Jessie Alden. I have a question to ask you, and it may sound a little strange."

Mrs. Pierce said, "What is it, Jessie?"

Jessie asked, "Did you ever think of having a magician at Alex's birthday?"

"It's funny you should ask," Mrs. Pierce said. "As a matter of fact, we did. Alex has always loved magic, so I called some of the magicians in the area."

"Was Cassandra the Great one of them?" Jessie asked.

"Yes, that name sounds familiar. I think she was," Mrs. Pierce said. "Why do you ask?"

"Oh, it's a long story," Jessie said. "There's just one other thing I was wondering. Did you tell the magicians what day you were planning to have the party?"

"Yes," said Mrs. Pierce. "That way they could let me know if they were available."

"Thanks so much for answering all my questions," Jessie said. "Um, have the police caught the burglar?"

"No, we haven't heard anything from the police." Mrs. Pierce sighed. "I guess they're still working on it."

"I hope they catch the burglar soon," Jessie said.

"So do I," Mrs. Pierce agreed. "And I hope your birthday business is going well," she added. "I've got to run. Good-bye!"

"Thanks," said Jessie as she hung up the phone. She quickly told the others what Mrs. Pierce had said.

"So Cassandra and her manager did know about both parties," Henry said.

"What I want to know," Violet said, "is, do they know we're doing a party tomorrow?"

The Aldens all looked at one another, wondering what the answer to that question could be.

Then Jessie added another question. "And if they do . . . what are they planning?"

CHAPTER 9

Setting a Trap

"Is there any way to find out if Cassandra and her manager know about tomorrow's party?" Benny asked.

"I remember the day we met the Woodruffs they said they were thinking of hiring her," Violet said.

"Yeah, and Mr. Woodruff kept saying he wanted to stick with her instead of us," Benny added.

"I think it's time for another phone call," said Henry, picking up the phone. He quickly dialed the Woodruffs' number.

"Hi, Mrs. Woodruff?" he said. "This is Henry Alden. I was just wondering . . . you mentioned that you'd thought of hiring Cassandra the Great to do Sara's party. . . . Did you actually hire her before you heard about us?"

"I didn't hire her, but I did call to see if she'd be available that day. I had a lot of different ideas — bowling, or a movie — before I hired you. But I did tell Cassandra that she was asking for too much money and I'd rather use you kids. She sounded pretty annoyed when I said that." Mrs. Woodruff chuckled.

"Really," Henry said.

"Why do you ask?" Mrs. Woodruff wanted to know. "There isn't any problem with tomorrow, is there?"

"Oh, no," Henry assured her. "Everything's all set to go. The cake's ready, the decorations have been made, the games have been planned."

"Great. Then I'll see you tomorrow afternoon," said Mrs. Woodruff.

"Okay!" Henry said, hanging up the phone.

Before he'd even said anything, the others could tell from the look on his face that he had bad news. "She said she *did* call Cassandra before she hired us. And when she told Cassandra she was thinking of using us instead of her, she said Cassandra got pretty mad."

"We've certainly heard a lot about Cassandra's bad temper," said Violet, her face worried.

"But would she get so angry she'd actually rob someone's house?" Benny wondered.

"I have an idea of how we can find out who the burglar is," said Henry.

"Are you thinking what I'm thinking?" Jessie asked. "Let's set a trap."

"Exactly," said Henry. "But I think we had better have a long talk with Grandfather first."

The Aldens showed up at the Woodruffs' house the next day, their arms laden with party supplies. The Woodruffs didn't notice, but Grandfather stayed parked outside while Sara led them down a long hallway into a large sunny room at the back of the house.

"This is our family room," she told them. "This is where the party is going to be."

Violet, Benny, and Sara got to work immediately, putting up the pictures of moons, planets, comets, and sparkly stars they'd painted.

Sara stood in the center of the room, turning slowly around. "Wow! This looks great! I feel like I'm in outer space!" She pretended to float around the room without gravity. Everyone laughed.

When the decorations had all been arranged, the children went into the dining room to set the table. Violet made sure they had all the supplies they'd need for the kids to make space helmets from paper bags. Henry made sure they had enough party favors for all the guests.

Sara's mother and father came down from upstairs and looked into the family room to see how the kids were doing.

"Your decorations are wonderful," Mrs. Woodruff said. "You're real artists."

"That's Violet," said Benny proudly.

"And Sara helped us a lot, too," Jessie added.

"Didn't they do a great job?" Mrs. Woodruff said, turning to her husband.

"Yeah, I guess it looks pretty good," Mr. Woodruff grumbled, without seeming to really mean it.

Just then the doorbell rang.

"My friends are here! My friends are here!" Sara cried, running to open the front door for them.

Mrs. Woodruff and the Aldens followed Sara, excited for the party to begin. But Mr. Woodruff went back upstairs as if he wasn't even interested in the party.

Several minutes later, all the guests had arrived. Sara led them into the family room.

"Wow!" several of the children said when they saw all the wonderful decorations.

"We're in outer space!" cried one little girl.

Violet had all of Sara's friends sit down

on the floor in a circle. The children had fun decorating the helmets with colored paper and markers, making moons and stars, and gluing them onto the paper bags.

Once the children were done with their space helmets, they took turns sitting in the rocket ship and pretending to fly. As each new pair of children sat in the cardboard box, Jessie would count down from twenty, shouting, "Blast off!" at the end.

While the children were enjoying themselves, Mrs. Woodruff walked around with her camera, taking pictures of all the kids.

Meanwhile, the Aldens had put their secret plan into action.

While Jessie, Violet, and Benny ran the birthday party, Henry had a special job. He was hiding in the Woodruffs' living room. Sara had mentioned that her house had a safe there like the other houses in the neighborhood, and the plan was for Henry to keep an eye on it through the whole party. If anyone tried to break into it, he'd be there to see.

Henry huddled behind the couch, which

sat in front of a large picture window. He peered around the end of the couch, his eyes on the front door. If anyone came in, he would see them, but they wouldn't be able to see him. Then he peered out between the curtains to Grandfather sitting in the passenger seat of his car and looking toward the house. They had agreed that if anyone suspicious showed up, Henry would signal Grandfather from the window.

Henry glanced around the elegant room at all the valuable pieces of art. He was sorry to be missing the party, which he could hear faintly down the hall in the family room. But he knew it was important that he stay where he was. Otherwise, the Aldens might never solve the mystery and find the thief. Henry wondered if it would turn out to be Cassandra, as they suspected.

For a long time nothing happened, and Henry began to wonder if maybe no one was going to show up. Maybe they'd been wrong, and the burglaries during their birthday parties had just been a coincidence.

At least they hadn't upset the Woodruffs by sharing their suspicions.

But suddenly Henry heard a sound at the front door. He held his breath and listened. Yes, it sounded as if someone was turning the knob. The door was slowly, slowly creaking open. All the guests had already arrived, so Henry knew it wasn't another guest.

Was it the thief?

Henry saw someone dressed in dark clothes enter the house very cautiously. At first Henry couldn't tell if it was a man or a woman. He saw the person look around to see if anyone was there. Luckily, he or she didn't spot Henry. Slowly, the person moved toward the living room, peering nervously from side to side. Henry was just about to shake the window curtains to signal Grandfather.

Then all at once Henry realized who the stranger was. Mr. Woodruff! But how could that be? Mr. Woodruff was upstairs, wasn't he? And why would he *sneak* into his own house? He certainly wouldn't be coming to steal his own things!

Henry didn't want Mr. Woodruff to find
him hiding behind a couch in the living
room. He figured it would be better to just
come out and explain what he was doing.
But just as Henry was about to emerge from
behind the couch, Mr. Woodruff passed the
living room and began moving down the
hall toward the family room. Henry spotted
the man's limp when he walked. But hadn't
Sara said her father didn't limp? And she
would know, wouldn't she?

Curious to see if he was going to join the
party, Henry followed Mr. Woodruff. But as
he stepped into the hall, the floor creaked
loudly, and Mr. Woodruff turned around.
Suddenly Henry was confused. The man
looked like Mr. Woodruff, but older. His
hair had more gray in it, and his face was
creased with lines.

"Who — who are you?" Henry asked,
startled.

"I knew I shouldn't come here, but — "
the man began.

Just then Sara came running down the
hall. "Uncle John!" she cried, giving the

man a big hug. "I was hoping you'd come!"

"Uncle John?" Henry repeated, confused.

Mrs. Woodruff was just behind Sara, and Bob Woodruff appeared on the stairs.

"John?" Bob Woodruff said. For the first time, Henry saw Mr. Woodruff smiling.

"Bob!" the other man said. "I've come to apologize."

"No, *I* should apologize to you," said Bob Woodruff, coming down the stairs and giving his brother a big hug. Henry watched Mrs. Woodruff smile broadly as the two men embraced. Sara clung to her uncle's waist, a big grin on her face, and Henry was *very* glad he hadn't signaled to Grandfather.

Violet, Jessie, and Benny emerged from the family room. After a few minutes, the Woodruffs became aware of the Aldens watching them. Mrs. Woodruff tried to explain.

"Bob and his brother, John, have always been quite close," she explained. "They were friends, golf buddies, business partners. He was like a second father to Sara. But about a year ago, they had a disagreement, something silly, really. But one thing led to another, and they stopped speaking. Both men are so proud — they each refused to be the one to admit he was wrong." Mrs. Woodruff paused, looking at the two brothers, who stood with their arms around each other, Sara happily nestled in between them.

"I thought your uncle John had . . . died," Jessie said to Sara.

"It felt almost as if he had," said Sara.

"I guess I was acting pretty ridiculous," Bob Woodruff admitted.

"No, *I* was," said John. "And I knew it, too. I just couldn't figure out how to admit it. And I felt especially badly because I knew Sara's birthday was coming up, and I hated to miss it. I've never missed any of your birthdays, cupcake," he said, ruffling her hair with his hand. Sara smiled up at him.

"I've been miserable since our fight," said Bob. "I just couldn't figure out how to make things right. I haven't been able to sleep at night, I've been so upset."

"Yes, and you've been taking it out on

everyone," said Mrs. Woodruff with a laugh.

"You sure have," Sara piped up.

"I'm sorry, honey," Bob Woodruff said, his voice kinder than the Aldens had ever heard it. "I'm not going to be that way anymore."

"And I've been lurking around your house, trying to get up my nerve to come in and apologize," said Uncle John. "I've even been following Sara and her friends around, thinking maybe if I talked to her, I could get up my nerve to talk to you, Bob."

"So that's it!" Benny shouted. Everyone turned to look at him. "You're the person who's been following us!"

"I thought you'd seen me," John Woodruff said.

"I did! I thought you were Sara's dad, but I knew there was something about you that was different. And then I got confused because you walk with a limp and he doesn't, right?" Benny said.

"Yes, that's right," said John. "I was injured falling off a horse many years ago, and my leg never healed properly."

"You were following the children?" Mrs. Woodruff asked, disbelieving.

"I know it sounds ridiculous," said John. "I finally decided that today, Sara's birthday, it was time to just come on in and apologize."

"Well, we're glad you did," said Mrs. Woodruff. "Now come join the party!"

All the Aldens and the Woodruffs returned to the family room, where the Aldens led the children in a few more games. Bob and John Woodruff sat side by side, smiling at Sara and her friends.

Soon it was almost time to serve the cake. "I'll go pour the juice and get everything ready," Jessie said, heading down the hall. She was passing through the living room when she stopped and gasped. She grabbed the window curtains and shook them frantically to signal Grandfather.

Standing in the living room was a tall person wearing a black mask, taking the Woodruffs' jewelry and stuffing it into a bag.

CHAPTER 10

The Trap Is Sprung!

"Help! Thief!" Jessie loudly screamed.

The person dropped the bag and ran out the other door of the living room.

"Stop!" Jessie screamed again, chasing after the burglar.

The person was almost to the front door, but just at that moment Grandfather opened the front door and stepped inside, blocking the stranger's way out. Henry and the others heard Jessie scream and came running. In no time they raced down the hall to the front door.

The person stopped and turned around, looking frantically from side to side for a way out. By now the Woodruffs and most of the children from the party had come into the hall as well.

The burglar realized there was nowhere to run, no way to escape.

"Cassandra, is that you?" Benny asked boldly.

The thief didn't answer. Instead, she slowly began to peel off her mask. When at last the Aldens could see her face, they couldn't believe their eyes.

"Ms. Fox?" Jessie asked.

"Aren't you the woman from the party store in town?" Mrs. Woodruff asked.

"Yes," Ms. Fox admitted. "I am."

"But what are you doing here? Are you the thief who's been breaking into houses in Greenfield? The Pierces' and the Graysons'?" Benny asked.

"Yes, I'm afraid I am," she said quietly.

"But — but . . . why?" Violet asked in a sad voice.

"Same reason most people steal," said Patti Fox. "For the money."

"Why was it always the houses where we were giving parties?" asked Henry.

"It was such a perfect plan," said Ms. Fox. "When you told me about the people who'd hired you, they always had lots of money and valuables in their homes. And with all the commotion of a birthday party going on in a separate part of the house — or even outside the house, like at the skating rink — I knew it would be easy to sneak in without anyone noticing."

"So whenever we told you we were planning a party — " Jessie began.

"I'd find out where and when, and I'd plan a robbery," Patti Fox said.

"How awful," Violet said sadly. "How did you open all those safes?"

"I've been doing this for a long time," Ms. Fox explained. "My father used to design safes, so I know all about them."

Just then, there was the sound of a siren outside as a police car pulled up, its lights flashing. While they'd all been talking, Bob Woodruff had called the police.

When the officers came into the house, they recognized Patti Fox immediately.

"We've been looking for you," the tall one said. "You're Patricia Fox, aren't you? Wanted for burglary in three states."

"Yes, that's me," Patti Fox said quietly.

In a few minutes, the officers had taken Patti Fox away.

Over the next few days, the Aldens got several more phone calls from people asking them to plan parties. They hated to turn anyone down, but it would be hard to prepare for so many parties and do a good job.

Then Violet came up with a good plan. Now that they knew Cassandra the Great wasn't a burglar or out to get them, she suggested they pay her a visit.

The children met Cassandra at her office in Greenfield. She was just as tall and beautiful as she looked onstage, but now she was dressed casually in jeans and a sweater.

"So what can I do for you?" she asked the

children once they were seated in her office. Her voice was businesslike, but she had a warm smile on her face. "You said on the phone you had a business proposition for me?"

"Yes," said Henry. "You entertain at a lot of birthday parties in Greenfield, and so do we. We don't want to compete with you, and we're getting so busy we can't keep up with all the parties. So we were thinking maybe we could work together."

"How would we do that?" Cassandra asked.

"We could do the preparation and the cleanup, make decorations, buy party favors and paper plates, things like that," Jessie explained. "We could make the cake and take care of all the refreshments. Maybe even plan a few small activities for the kids to start with. But you could do most of the entertainment with your magic act."

"I see," said Cassandra thoughtfully. She drummed her fingers on the desk for a couple of minutes as she mulled over what the Aldens had just suggested.

"I like the idea," she said at last. "I've never been interested in handling the food or the cleanup, but some parents have asked me to. I think working with you kids might be just the answer."

"Great!" said Jessie.

"I should be honest with you," Cassandra said. "I was worried about your party service taking some of my business. I depend on that business for a part of my income, and it hasn't been doing so well lately. Several parents I spoke with chose you over me. I was starting to wonder who you Aldens were and what was so special about you."

"Is that why you tore down our posters?" Benny asked.

Cassandra's face turned red. "That wasn't me — that was my manager. He tends to get a little carried away sometimes. I'm sorry about that."

"We thought maybe you recognized our name when we came up to volunteer in your show," said Jessie.

"Yes, I did." Cassandra laughed. "I was

quite surprised when you said your name was Alden, and I wondered how a bunch of kids could be causing me so much trouble!"

"We're not just kids, we're detectives!" Benny said, drawing himself up to his full height.

The others laughed and Jessie mussed Benny's hair.

"Detectives, and great party planners. Working together might solve a lot of problems," said Cassandra.

"That way you wouldn't have to get rid of us," Benny said.

"Get rid of you?" Cassandra repeated, confused.

"Yeah, you know, like you told your manager when you were in the party store," Benny explained.

Cassandra looked puzzled for a second, and then she burst out laughing. She laughed for several moments, while the Aldens just looked at one another.

"What's so funny?" Benny asked at last.

Cassandra stopped laughing and caught her breath. "You heard me say something about 'getting rid of' someone and you assumed it was you?" she asked.

"Well, yes," Jessie said.

"I wasn't talking about you," Cassandra said. "I was talking about Larry and Betty."

"Who are they?" asked Benny.

"My doves! I've been having trouble with the trick where I make them disappear. I told my manager that if I couldn't get it to work, I'd have to get rid of the birds and return them to the animal trainer."

Cassandra was no longer the only one laughing. The Aldens couldn't help but laugh over the misunderstanding. Cassandra leaned down and reached under her desk.

"I'm glad to know you weren't planning to get rid of us," said Benny.

"Rid of you?" Cassandra laughed as she drew something out from under the desk. "It would take more than a magician to get rid of the best detectives in Greenfield," she said, placing a white dove on Benny's head.

GERTRUDE CHANDLER WARNER discovered when she was teaching that many readers who like an exciting story could find no books that were both easy and fun to read. She decided to try to meet this need, and her first book, *The Boxcar Children*, quickly proved she had succeeded.

Miss Warner drew on her own experiences to write the mystery. As a child she spent hours watching trains go by on the tracks opposite her family home. She often dreamed about what it would be like to set up housekeeping in a caboose or freight car—the situation the Alden children find themselves in.

While the mystery element is central to each of Miss Warner's books, she never thought of them as strictly juvenile mysteries. She liked to stress the Aldens' independence and resourcefulness and their solid New England devotion to using up and making do. The Aldens go about most of their adventures with as little adult supervision as possible—something else that delights young readers.

Miss Warner lived in Putnam, Connecticut, until her death in 1979. During her lifetime, she received hundreds of letters from girls and boys telling her how much they liked her books.